Y y

Yesterday and the Letter Y

Alphabet Friends

by Cynthia Klingel and Robert B. Noyed

The Child's World®

Published in the United States of America
by The Child's World®
P.O. Box 326
Chanhassen, MN 55317-0326
800-599-READ
www.childsworld.com

The Child's World®: Mary Berendes, Publishing Director

Editorial Directions, Inc.: E. Russell Primm, Editorial
Director; Emily Dolbear, Line Editor; Ruth Martin,
Editorial Assistant; Linda S. Koutris, Photo Researcher
and Selector

Photographs ©: Ryan McVay/Photodisc/Getty Images;
Cover & 21; Ryan McVay/Photodisc/Picture Quest: 9;
Lester Lefkowitz/Corbis: 10; Photodisc/Getty Images:
13; Paul Barton/Corbis: 14; Barbara Penoyar/
Photodisc/Getty Images: 17; Rick Gayle/Corbis: 18.

Library of Congress Cataloging-in-Publication Data
Klingel, Cynthia Fitterer.
  Yesterday and the letter Y / by Cynthia Klingel and
Robert B. Noyed.
      p. cm. — (Alphabet readers)
Summary: A simple story about children in a class
sharing what they did yesterday introduces the letter "y".
  ISBN 1-59296-115-0 (Library Bound : alk. paper)
[1. Memory—Fiction. 2. Alphabet.] I. Noyed, Robert B.,
ill. II. Title. III. Series.
  PZ7.K6798Ye 2003
  [E]—dc21   2003006613

Note to parents and educators:
The first skill children acquire before becoming successful readers is individual letter recognition. The Alphabet Friends series has been created with the needs of young learners in mind. Each engaging book begins by showing the difference between the capital letter and the lowercase letter. In each of the books on the vowels and the consonants c and g, children are introduced to the different sounds that the letter can make. Finally, children see that the letters can be found at the beginning of a word, in the middle of a word, and in most cases, at the end of a word.

Following the introduction, children meet their Alphabet Friends. The friend in each story encounters many words that include the featured letter of that book. Each noun that begins with the title letter is highlighted in red with the initial letter of the word in bold. Above the word is a rebus drawing that establishes a strong picture cue.

At the end of each book, we have included three words lists. Can your young learners find all the words in each book with the title letter in them?

Let's learn about the letter **Y.**

The letter **Y** can look like this: **Y.**

The letter **Y** can also look like this: **y.**

The letter **y** can be at the beginning of a word, like yard.

yard

The letter **y** can be in the middle of a word, like volleyball.

volle**y**ball

The letter **y** can be at the end of a word, like library.

librar**y**

The teacher asked the class, "What

did you do **y**esterday?" Everyone had

a chance to share a memory.

Yolanda said that **y**esterday she came

home from Wyoming. She was on

a trip with her family. It was a long

way to Wyoming. **Y**olanda had fun

with her family.

Billy said that **y**esterday he played in his

yard. Many other boys came to play.

They played in the **y**ard all day.

13

Anthony said that **y**esterday he

watched baseball. He watched the

game on television with his Uncle

Vinny. Uncle Vinny yelled when there

was a good play.

Yukio said that **y**esterday he babysat

his younger brother. His younger brother

is very active! **Y**ukio's brother kept him

quite busy.

Kyle said that **y**esterday he went to

the store. He wanted to spend the

money he earned mowing **y**ards.

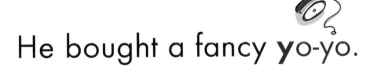

He bought a fancy **y**o-yo.

"You did many things **y**esterday," said the

teacher. Everyone had a memory to share.

What did you do **y**esterday?

Fun Facts

When you think of a **y**ard, do you think of a grassy area near a house or school? That is one kind of **y**ard, but there are also navy **y**ards and railroad **y**ards. These **y**ards are used to build, store, and repair ships and trains. And, of course, there is the famous Scotland **Y**ard! Scotland **Y**ard, the headquarters of London's police force, was named for a nearby medieval palace. Kings and queens of Scotland lived in this palace when visiting London.

People all around the world play with **y**o-yos. **Y**o-yos have even been in space! In both 1985 and 1992, astronauts brought **y**o-yos onto their space shuttles to study gravity. **Y**o-yos became popular in the United States in 1930. Donald Duncan, who owned a company that made **y**o-yos, began holding **y**o-yo demonstrations and contests across the country. Luck, Wisconsin, has been the "**y**o-yo capital of the world" since the Duncan **Y**o-Yo Company moved there in 1946.

To Read More

About the Letter Y

Flanagan, Alice K. *Yum!: The Sound of Y.* Chanhassen, Minn.: The Child's World, 2000.

About Yards

Herman, Gail, and Jerry Smith (illustrator). *Buried in the Backyard.* New York: Kane Press, 2003.

Modarressi, Mitra. *Yard Sale!* New York: DK Publishing, 2000.

Quinn, Greg Henry, and Lena Shiffman (illustrator). *The Garden in Our Yard.* New York: Scholastic Inc., 1995.

About Yo-yos

Cassidy, John. *The Klutz Yo-Yo Books.* Palo Alto, Calif.: Klutz, Inc., 1998.

Roper, Ingrid. *Yo-Yos: Tricks to Amaze Your Friends.* New York: HarperCollins Juvenile Books, 2001.

Words with Y

Words with **Y** at the Beginning

yard

yards

yelled

yesterday

Yolanda

you

younger

yo-yo

Yukio

Words with **Y** in the Middle

babysat

boys

everyone

kyle

played

volleyball

wyoming

yo-yo

Words with **Y** at the End

anthony

billy

busy

day

family

fancy

library

many

memory

money

play

they

very

vinny

way

yesterday

About the Authors

Cynthia Klingel has worked as a high school English teacher and an elementary teacher. She is currently the curriculum director for a Minnesota school district. Cynthia Klingel lives with her family in Mankato, Minnesota.

Robert B. Noyed started his career as a newspaper reporter. Since then, he has worked in communications and public relations for a Minnesota school district for more than fourteen years. Robert B. Noyed lives with his family in Brooklyn Center, Minnesota.